STRANDED

STRANDED

Jocelyn Shipley

orca soundings

ORCA BOOK PUBLISHERS

Published in Canada and the United States in 2020 by Orca Book Publishers.
orcabook.com

Library and Archives Canada Cataloguing in Publication
Title: Stranded / Jocelyn Shipley.
Names: Shipley, Jocelyn, author.
Series: Orca soundings.
Description: Series statement: Orca soundings
Identifiers: Canadiana (print) 20200176013 | Canadiana (ebook) 20200176021 |
ISBN 9781459823891 (softcover) | ISBN 9781459823907 (PDF) |
ISBN 9781459823914 (EPUB)
Classification: LCC PS8587.H563 S73 2020 | DDC jc813/.6—dc23

Library of Congress Control Number: 2020930591

Summary: In this high-interest accessible novel for teen readers, after a string
of really bad luck, a teenage boy takes a woman up on her generous offer of free
room and board. But he soon learns that things are not as they seem.

Orca Book Publishers is committed to reducing the consumption
of nonrenewable resources in the making of our books. We make
every effort to use materials that support a sustainable future.

Orca Book Publishers gratefully acknowledges the support for its
publishing programs provided by the following agencies: the Government
of Canada, the Canada Council for the Arts and the Province of British
Columbia through the BC Arts Council and the Book Publishing Tax Credit.

Edited by Tanya Trafford
Design by Ella Collier
Cover images by Unsplash.com/Nathan Dumlao
and Gettyimages.ca/sabelskaya (front) and
Shutterstock.com/Krasovski Dmitri (back)

Printed and bound in Canada.

23 22 21 20 • 1 2 3 4

For my family

Chapter One

Today is the six-month anniversary of my girlfriend's death. It will be tough to get through. But I made a promise to honor Fern's memory and turn my life around, and I'm going to keep it.

Sure, I screwed up big-time after she died. But look how far I've come. Three months ago I started off as a dishwasher at Pepper & Pie restaurant. I worked my way up and now I'm a shift manager, and I help train staff.

There's a new girl working this morning. Amena is from Syria and hasn't been here long. Her English isn't great, but I think she understands me okay. I explain that customers order and pay at the counter, and then we give them a number to put on their table. When their food is ready, she should take it to the table with that number.

When the next order comes up, she looks unsure. "Go ahead and serve it to table ten," I tell her. "Over there."

She picks up the burger-combo plate and heads to the right table. But she walks like she's scared of dropping it. Like she's scared of everything.

The other servers rush past and around her. Pepper & Pie is always busy, and we have to be fast. Super fast. But this is Amena's first day, so I'll wait and tell her later that she'll need to move more quickly.

The guy at table ten isn't happy with the slow service. "Hey, fatso!" he shouts. "Move it!"

Amena lowers her head and hurries a bit. But when she finally reaches his table, she sets the plate down too hard. Some of the soup slops over the edge of the bowl. Some of the fries go flying onto the floor.

"Freakin' terrorist!" the guy yells. "Go back where you came from!"

Amena freezes.

The guy turns to all the customers watching. "Immigrants are ruining this country!"

I look around for my boss, but Jasmine's out back somewhere.

I can't just stand there. I take a deep breath and say in a calm voice, "Sir? If you don't stop insulting my co-worker, I'll have to ask you to leave."

"Oh yeah?" He stands and gets all in my face. I can smell that he's been drinking. "Be my guest, big man."

He doesn't leave, and I don't know what to do. Jasmine has warned me twice already not to get into it with customers.

The first time was because I told this couple that left without eating the food they'd ordered that they were being wasteful. I asked if they were aware that street kids would be grateful for even half that much food.

The second time was because I told a mom to stop calling her little kid a *useless piece of crap* after he spilled his drink. Then she really went off on him, and he started crying. I couldn't take it and said she shouldn't be allowed to be a parent.

When Jasmine called me into her office that time, she said, "Look, I like you, Kipp. You're a good worker, reliable and responsible. But I can't have you mouthing off to customers. This is your last warning."

I know I should let Jasmine handle this situation. But I don't want to go look for her and leave Amena alone with the rude guy. So I say, "With respect, sir. We don't tolerate racist comments here. Please leave."

Amena doesn't make a sound, but tears flood her face. "Take a break," I tell her. "And please ask Jasmine to come out here."

Amena nods, but as she turns to go, the guy grabs at her hijab. It's like he wants to rip it right off her head.

I reach out to stop him. Amena runs. The guy laughs. "She your girlfriend? You got a thing for terrorists?"

I give him a push toward the door. "Out before I call the cops." Wrong move. He's way bigger than me. And he's pissed off.

He pushes back. "You little shit!"

I punch him in the gut.

The guy doubles over for a second and then quickly leaves. On his way out he threatens to charge me with assault. Great. Just what I need.

Jasmine appears just in time to see our fight. She orders me into her office. "For god's sake, Kipp," she says. "What were you thinking?"

What I was thinking was that the guy was an asshole. "Sorry. He was being a jerk. He insulted Amena and then called her a terrorist. He even tried to rip her hijab off. I asked him to leave, but he refused."

Jasmine sighs and shakes her head. "I understand, but you can't hit a customer!"

"I know. Sorry. It won't happen again."

"Darn right it won't. You're fired."

"*What?*"

"Kipp, you've been warned more than once. That guy could call the cops. I can't have my staff assaulting customers. And what if somebody took a video and posts it?"

Somebody probably already has. Yeah, I definitely should have thought of those things. But still. "Customers shouldn't be racist. Or sexist."

Jasmine gives me a sympathetic look. I know she knows from experience exactly what I mean. "Agree. It's wrong, but violence is never the answer. I'm sorry, but I can't keep you on."

I stand there trying not to yell. Or beg for another chance.

"Go," she says. "And don't bother asking for your pay. Or a reference. You had your chance, Kipp. I have to protect myself and my business."

Then I do yell. "Hey, you can't do that! You have to pay me out."

"Consider yourself lucky I don't give that guy your name if he comes back."

As I storm out of her office, she calls after me, "Word of advice? Get some help with your impulse-control issues."

I'd like to tell her why I sometimes lash out. How it wasn't fair that Fern died. How it wouldn't have happened if I'd been there at the party that night. How I struggle every single day with grief and guilt.

But that won't get me my job back.

And nothing will get Fern back.

Chapter Two

I can't believe I just got fired. How did that happen? Because I was upset about it being the anniversary of Fern's death and couldn't control myself.

I should have handled the situation better.

Crap. I was doing so well. And now I don't have a job.

There's nothing to do but go home. I have to take two buses and then walk ten blocks to get there.

When I reach the rundown house I share, I stop short. Oh no. No, no, no!

Piles of bursting garbage bags and household junk litter the front porch. A real-estate agent is hammering a *For Sale* sign into our front yard.

"What's going on?" I ask. The agent looks all rich and smug in his leather jacket and limited-edition sneakers.

He pulls out his phone and starts taking pictures. Probably the "before" shots, because this is a sketchy area that's gentrifying. A couple other houses on the street have already been sold and demolished. Monster homes now stand in their places.

"Obvious, isn't it?" the agent asks. "Landlord is cashing out."

"How much?"

"We're asking low, just a million. For the land. But it will probably go for more."

The prices in this city are insane, which makes rents impossible too. Which is why seven of us have been stuffed into this little shack. For three hundred bucks a month I get to unroll my sleeping bag on the floor in a room with two other guys.

"Better grab your gear and get lost," the agent says. "Duke's on his way. Says you owe rent."

"Not me." I hurry up the rickety steps and rip through the pile of bags. Whoever filled them didn't bother to tie them, making it easier to find what belongs to me. I try the door of the house, but my key doesn't work.

"Lock's changed," the agent says. "Sorry."

"What? But we've got until the end of the month."

"Sorry," he says again. "Duke doesn't care. Says you guys haven't paid."

Great. I knew I shouldn't have given my rent money to Wes. He's the one who let me stay here and who collects from all of us every month. I just assumed he'd paid Duke.

But of course he probably smoked, drank or snorted away my rent money. It's happened before.

He promised never again, and I believed him. Man, I'm such an idiot.

"You must have known this place would go up for sale," the agent says. "And I understand you don't have a lease?"

"Yeah, no lease. Duke was just letting us live here month to month until he decided to sell." What a disaster. None of us have any options for other places to live.

"Heads up," the agent says. "Here he is."

I see Duke's red vintage Mustang speeding down the street. I grab my two pathetic bags of stuff and run.

Too slow. Duke pulls over and jumps out of his car. He's not a big guy, but he's made of muscle. He grabs my arm to stop me. I lose hold of one of the bags, and my clothes spill out onto the sidewalk. "You owe me!" he snarls.

"No, I don't. I paid Wes."

"But that druggie didn't pay me." He twists my arm up behind my back.

I yelp in pain and drop the other bag.

"Hey, leave the kid alone," the agent yells. Thank God he's here. Otherwise Duke would have given me a beating like he gave Wes that other time we owed money.

"Somebody needs to pay." Duke twists my arm higher. It hurts like hell, but if I struggle he'll break it.

"Forget it, Duke," the agent says, coming over. "You're going to make so much money, what's a few hundred to you?"

Duke lets me go but says, "Don't think you're safe." He kicks my stuff around. "I'll be looking for all of you."

I gather everything up, only realizing now that my sleeping bag must still be in the house. There are big muddy footprints all over my one good shirt. I fold it and my one good pair of pants, which are also a mess, back into a garbage bag.

Can I ever get them clean enough to wear again? Does it even matter? Because how will I land interviews with no reference from my last place of employment?

I knot both bags so the clothes can't spill out again. My arms ache as I lug them to the park, where I sit down on a bench. I sit on this same bench whenever I've got nowhere else to be. It's my special place to think about Fern. And, okay, sometimes I talk to her in my head.

Fern moved to Helston Bay in twelfth grade, and I fell for her right away. She was so full of life. She had goals and plans. She wanted to be a vet. I wanted to go to cooking school. Meeting her was the best thing that ever happened to me. We were going to get out of town and succeed together.

And then there was that bush party last May. If only I'd gone with her. But the party was at this property on the other side of the bay. A long drive but a short trip by water. Everybody was going in this older guy's fishing boat. Everybody except me.

I'm scared of boats. Fern didn't know that because I didn't want her to think I was a wimp. Instead of admitting my fear, I lied and said I had to work. I didn't want to talk about why I'm scared of boats.

When I was four years old, my mom took me out in a canoe. She wanted to paddle to this island in the middle of Dogwood Lake. But she was wasted, and we tipped over. I wasn't wearing a life jacket, and I almost drowned.

After that I had to go live with my uncle. He didn't want me. But my mom was in rehab, so it was that or foster care. The good thing is I learned to look after myself early. If I wanted to eat, I had to make the food. If I wanted clean clothes, I had to do the laundry. If I wanted money for stuff, I had to earn it.

I couldn't wait to get out of there.

And after Fern died, I did. I couldn't face her family or her funeral. So I ran away to the city and fell apart. For the first three months I was a wreck.

Then I found this youth shelter, Cedarvale. They helped me turn things around, and I vowed to make something of my life for Fern's sake.

I really thought I was getting there. I'd been planning to come to the bench today to tell her how good I'm doing. How I have a job and a place to live.

So much for that.

Chapter Three

What am I going to do? I'd like to get drunk or something, but I've already screwed up today. I don't want to make another bad choice. I might feel better for a while, but it wouldn't solve my problem.

Winter's coming, and I don't have any money saved. I was barely making enough to feed myself and pay rent. I'm stuck, and I need help.

All I can think to do is go back to Cedarvale. I hate to show up there as such a failure, but if I don't, I'll be living on the street. And I won't survive that hell again.

I pick up my pathetic bags of secondhand stuff and start walking. At least the shelter's not too far from here. I just hope it isn't full.

On my way out of the park I see this lady who looks kind of familiar. And also really sad. She's wearing a fancy black coat and high boots. She's carrying a huge leather purse that's more like a briefcase.

At first I can't remember where I've seen her before. And then it hits me. "Hey," I say. "Front-desk lady?" It's her upscale clothes that remind me. She used to volunteer at Cedarvale and was always wearing business suits because she came in after work. Which made her stand out from everybody else there. "You're Reba, right?"

She stops and stares at me.

"You still volunteer at Cedarvale? You always used to smile at me." She used to talk to me too. Always wanted to know how things were going. I realize that her eyes are wet, like she's been crying. I set my garbage bags down at my feet. "You okay?"

She pulls a tissue from her purse and wipes her eyes. "No, I don't have time to volunteer now. And yes, sorry, I'm fine. I'm just really missing my son today."

"Aw, I'm sorry." I know how it feels to be missing somebody. The thought of Fern being gone is heartbreaking. "Where does your son live?"

"He's away at school in England, and I haven't seen him for over a year."

"He doesn't come home for holidays? You can't go visit?"

She tenses. "Well, it's a long trip, and we're both super busy."

"You can't Skype or something?"

"Of course, but the time difference makes it difficult." She takes a closer look at me. "You're Kipp? How are you doing?"

"Yeah, that's me." I kick at my bags of stuff. "Honestly? I've been better."

"Oh, but I remember now. The last time I saw you, you'd just landed a good restaurant job. And I think you were saving up to go back to school?"

"Yup. I was planning on cooking school, but I just got fired. And the house I was sharing with some guys from Cedarvale is suddenly for sale, so we've been evicted."

"Yikes. That's awful. You didn't have a lease?"

"Yeah, it sucks, and no, no lease." Something about how nice she's being makes me add, "Yesterday I was okay, and now I'm screwed. I was just heading back to Cedarvale, actually. See if they'll take me in again."

She looks up at the sky, which is clouding over. It will probably start raining soon. And then for the next five months. "You know what?" she says. "Since my son's away, I've got lots of space. And I work really long hours, so it would be good to have someone around to look after things. You could stay in his room."

Did she really offer to let me live in her house? "Seriously?"

"Well, just until you can make other arrangements. Interested?"

"Are you sure?"

"Yes, of course. And I could pay you a little to do some cleaning and yard work. To help you get back on track."

She has to be joking. We hardly know each other. But on the other hand, anybody who volunteered at Cedarvale must be a good person. They have to have police background checks and all that stuff. So I say, "Hey, I could cook for you too! Make dinner every night. I'm pretty good."

"Oh, that would be wonderful. Sounds like we have a deal?"

Wow. That was fast. Too fast? Maybe I should slow down? I don't want to lose this chance, if it's for real. But I'm not stupid.

One thing I've learned is that I have to protect myself. Nobody's going to do it for me. "Um," I say. "Two questions. First, why would you want to help me?"

"Because you had a good reputation at Cedarvale, and I know how hard you're trying. And I know how tough it is out there." Drops of rain start to fall. She pulls an umbrella from her briefcase purse, opens it and holds it over us both. "And I really would like somebody in the house when I'm not home. I did have a guy, but he got a job and moved out. You'd be doing me a favor."

That makes sense. "You've had other kids living with you?"

"Helping kids in need is the least I can do, considering how much I have. I know I'm privileged, and I want to pay it forward."

"Okay, great. So my second question is, what's the catch?"

She smiles and shakes her head. "No catch."

"There's always a catch when something sounds too good to be true."

"Right. And I'm glad you asked, because it shows you're responsible and try to think things through." She makes direct eye contact, and her expression goes serious. "The catch is, I do have one strict rule. No drugs. No substance abuse of any kind. You okay with that?"

I nod. "Been clean and sober three months now." And I plan to stay that way, given what happened to Fern.

"Congratulations. I'm happy to hear that." The rain starts to falls harder, and Reba shifts her umbrella to shelter us better. "So you'll come live at my place and work for me?"

Should I go for it or not? Is this a scam of some kind? Is she going to sell me into the sex trade? Does she plan to have sex with me herself? Gross! I can't believe I even thought that. But you never know.

She's not giving off any evil vibes though. She's very motherly. And I've always wanted a mother.

Winter's coming. I'm broke and have no job and no place to live.

Deep down I know Fern wouldn't be mad at me for not being at the party, but she would be mad if I don't keep trying to reach my goal. Living at Reba's house would probably be a good step on that road.

What could possibly go wrong?

Lots of things, but it's the best offer I've got.

Is it too good to be true?

Maybe.

Or maybe not.

Maybe it's my lucky break.

Chapter Four

Reba's Lexus SUV is parked on a side street a few blocks away. There's a lot of traffic, and it's raining hard now. She's a bit of a nervous driver, so I don't distract her by talking. Instead I take in the details of her car. It's all shiny and smooth. Heated leather seats and an incredible sound system. Sweet!

When we get to her house, on the west side of the city, I'm even more impressed. "Nice place!"

"Thanks. I'm lucky I bought it twenty years ago, when my son was a baby. Couldn't afford it now." She parks and leads me to a side entrance and downstairs to a self-contained suite. "This is Ben's space," she says. "Yours for now. Come and go as you like. I'll find you a spare key."

"Oh, wow! This is amazing," I say. There's even my own bathroom! "But do you really want me here? 'Cause you could rent this out for big bucks."

"I know, but I'd have to pack up all of Ben's things, and I want to keep it ready for him."

I set my garbage bags on a plaid duvet covering a huge platform bed. "Thank you so much," I say. "I really appreciate this. And don't worry—I'll leave if your son comes home for the holidays or something. I won't make trouble."

"Good to know, but I have a guest room too. And it's not likely Ben will show up anyway. He has so little free time with studying and all." She starts back up the stairs. "Now come see the rest of the house."

There's a huge living room with a fireplace, a dining room, an office, three bedrooms and three bathrooms. But it's the kitchen that really takes my breath away. Maple cabinets, black granite counters and stainless-steel appliances. "Oh yeah," I say, trying to sound casual. "I can cook in here." Like I've ever cooked anywhere better. Or even half as nice.

"I guess we should have stopped for groceries." Reba checks the fridge. "But there's lots of veggies and some soba noodles, if you're still offering to make dinner."

"You bet." I wash my hands and put water on to boil. I find sesame oil, five-star spice, a bamboo chopping board and a professional-quality knife. She really has the best of everything.

Reba perches on a counter stool while I chop green onions, ginger, mushrooms, broccoli and snow peas. "I know you spent some time at Cedarvale," she says. "But how did you end up there? What's your story? If you don't mind me asking."

I seed a red pepper. "I don't mind. I mean, it's only fair to be straight with you since you're being so generous taking me in and all. But it's kind of painful, you know?"

"I'm listening," she says.

"My girlfriend accidentally overdosed at a party, and it's my fault because I wasn't there. I guess nobody noticed when she passed out, and by the time they did, it was too late. She didn't make it. But if I'd been there with her, I'd have been paying attention. I'd have gotten her help in time."

Reba rests her elbows on the counter and her chin in her hands. "Where were you?"

"At home playing video games." No need to tell Reba about being scared of boats. Or why. I open the fridge, randomly reach for a can of soda, then quickly put it back. "Sorry."

"No, no, help yourself. Please feel at home here."

"Thanks." I open the soda and take a drink. "This stuff is full of sugar, but it tastes great, and it keeps me off beer."

"I certainly hope so. About the beer, I mean." She gives me a look. "What happened after your girlfriend died?"

"I couldn't face Fern's family or our friends because I should have been there. I didn't even go to her funeral. I hitched to Vancouver and lived on the streets for the summer, off my head most of the time. Then I found Cedarvale and got clean. I vowed to make something of my life to honor Fern. And things were going pretty good until today."

"I'm very sorry about your girlfriend. That is so incredibly sad."

"Yeah," I say. "Yeah. She didn't even use drugs much at all. Neither of us did. She just tried something at a party. For fun. And look what happened."

"Right," Reba says. "Bad stuff happens."

I turn away to add the noodles to the boiling water. Then I add oil to the wok I've preheated and toss in the vegetables. They give off a delicious aroma as they sizzle.

"Anyway, what about you?" I stir the veggies fast so they cook evenly. "Besides volunteering at Cedarvale."

Reba slips off the stool to set out noodle bowls and chopsticks. "I'm a tax lawyer. Boring, but it pays well."

"Hey, money is good." I drain the noodles, take the wok off the heat and add a handful of cashews and a splash of soy sauce. "Let's eat."

"You must have cooked a lot at home?" Reba asks after the first few bites. "This is amazing!"

"Yeah, I kind of had to. I mostly taught myself, growing up. And then Cedarvale got me into a basic skills course, and I learned a lot more at Pepper & Pie."

"Well, you'll be a famous chef someday, I'm sure."

"Thanks. That's the plan." If I can stick to it. Won't be easy. But I made that vow.

After dinner I clean up the kitchen. Reba asks for my phone number so she can contact me if needed. She leaves for work early and stays late, so she'll text me to tell me what my jobs are each day. Except I don't even have a phone. Too expensive.

If Jasmine wanted to get in touch with me, she had to call my roommate Wes and hope he'd give me a message. Which was a real pain, because Wes was so unreliable. Jasmine learned not to change my shifts or try to call me in if somebody was sick.

"You don't have a phone?" Reba says. "You're joking, right?" Like I just don't want to give her my number or something.

"Can't afford one."

"Well, that won't do." She goes to her office, comes back with an iPhone and hands it to me. "This is an extra I keep for backup. It's basic, but it works fine, and it has a good plan."

I hold the phone in my hand and stare at it for a moment. Then I try to give it back to her. "Thanks, but there's no way I can afford this."

"It comes with the job. So please, just take it. I need to be able to reach you."

"Oh," I say. I am not really sure how to react. "Okay then. So...uh...I guess you already have the number?"

"I do. And mine's in the contacts."

Reba returns to her office to work, and I go downstairs to Ben's room. Did she really just give me a phone? How cool is that?

And I can't wait to have a shower in my own private, clean bathroom and sleep in a real bed with two pillows and without my roommates farting and snoring.

Just before I fall asleep, I get a text from Reba. **Welcome Kipp!**

Then another. **Pressure washer in garage. Pls clean driveway and back patio tomorrow.**

And then one more. **Don't forget the rule. No drugs!**

Chapter Five

I love living at Reba's house. I've never had it so good. Her son's room is awesome, and I wonder if he knows how lucky he is. Besides living here and having Reba for a mom, the clothes he's left in his closet are all more stylish than anything I've ever owned. Don't know why he didn't take them to college, but he's probably got even cooler stuff there.

I don't see much of Reba. She's gone when I get up in the morning, and after dinner she spends the evenings in her office. During the day she texts me what she wants done. So far it's been stuff like end-of-season garden cleanup, washing windows and clearing the gutters. I still have lots of time for video games, Netflix, looking up recipes online and cooking.

I try hard to impress Reba with my culinary skills. She has her office assistant do the shopping online, and when the groceries are delivered, I unpack them and put them away. Reba likes organic produce, fair-trade coffee, humanely raised, antibiotic-free meat and sustainable seafood. And she can afford it.

We eat so well I feel guilty. I can't help thinking about all the homeless people lined up at soup kitchens and picking food out of trash cans. Like I used to do.

Even though she works the rest of the time, Reba does usually eat dinner with me. She tells me what a great job I'm doing around the yard. She always loves what I cook and asks every day what I want put on the shopping list.

And she also asks if I'm obeying her no drugs rule. Yeah, I am.

The only thing I don't like about my posh new life is the loneliness. Reba's great, but she's more like a parent than a friend. I miss Fern so much. And I'm so starved for the company of people my own age that I almost miss the guys I was sharing the house with.

Out here in this exclusive suburb where Reba lives, it's empty and quiet. I don't see any kids. I don't see anybody around at all.

And then one day when I'm raking up the last leaves from the big maple in the front yard, this girl comes by. She's maybe seventeen or so, really pretty, with long dark hair and dark eyes. "Hey," she says. "You work here?"

How did she know that? This could be my family home. "Um, yeah."

"I'm Lin Cheng. Have you seen my brother?"

I stop raking. "What?"

"His name is Jian, and he was living and working here. He was supposed to meet me last weekend and he didn't show up, and his phone is out of service."

I think about that for a minute. Reba did say she'd helped other kids. Maybe this girl's brother was one of them? And I remember Reba saying she'd had someone here but he got a job and moved out. "Sorry, haven't seen him."

I go back to my raking. Man, there's a ton of leaves. Reba's house has a huge yard with so many trees. But it's a beautiful late-fall day, perfect for working outdoors.

"Jian wouldn't just disappear. Our parents kicked him out a while back, but he's always stayed in contact with me. And the last I heard, he was going out on that lady's boat."

"What lady?"

"The lady who lives here. He said she was taking him to Salish Island or somewhere like that."

Reba has a boat? She's never mentioned one, but of course she'd have a boat. She has everything. I stuff the pile of leaves I've raked into a yard bag. "Well, if your brother was here, he was gone before I came."

"He was definitely here, and he was so happy about this job. He'd been sleeping on the street for months until she offered him work and a place to live. So why would he disappear?"

"Don't know." So many reasons. Or maybe just one, like Reba's rule. Maybe this Jian pissed her off by drinking or doing drugs or something. "Maybe he just ran away?"

"He wouldn't do that. He was saving to get his own place and go back to school."

"Maybe he got a job and moved out, and he'll contact you soon?"

"No. Not possible. Could you do me a favor?"

"Depends. What is it?"

"Could you let me in to have a look around?"

Seriously? "No, sorry." It's not like Reba's ever said not to let anybody in. But why should I trust this girl? What if this is a scam?

What if she wants in to scope the place out? Maybe take photos and text them to somebody who'll come by later with a truck? Somebody who'll beat me up and drive away with everything?

"Please? I'm so worried about Jian."

She seems really upset. But maybe she's just a good actor. "Sorry, can't do that."

I can't lose this job. Not with nowhere else to live and Duke the landlord looking for me. And what if it was Duke who sent her?

Or what if Reba sent her? What if Reba is testing me? She said she wanted somebody looking after things while she's at work. What if she's trying to find out if I'd let a stranger into her house?

"You should probably go now," I tell the girl. But I kind of wish she'd stay, just so I'd have someone to talk to. Well, if she was saying normal things, not crazy stuff.

"Okay, I get it," she says. "But could you just have a look around for me?"

"What would I look for?"

"Anything suspicious. Like, maybe some of his clothes are still there, or I don't know, maybe he's locked up in the basement or something?"

I burst out laughing. "Yeah, I'm pretty sure I'd know if there was a kid tied up down there."

"Please?"

"Not happening."

"Do you have a brother?" she asks.

"Nope."

"Okay, well, what if your best friend went missing? Wouldn't you want somebody to help?"

Wrong thing for her to say. My best friend is dead. And I wasn't there to help her. "You're keeping me from my work. Gotta finish this raking and make dinner."

The girl starts to cry, tears streaming down her face. "If you do find out something," she chokes out, "I work at Happy Cookies, my parents' bakery, after school and on weekends." As she turns to walk away, she adds, "Please, just look around. Anything would help. Anything at all."

Chapter Six

I can't stop thinking about that girl who came by. Lin Cheng. What a strange story about her brother. I don't know whether to believe her or not.

And okay, I'm also still thinking about her because I kind of liked her. Which is weird too, because I haven't been interested in other girls much since Fern died. And I've had lots of chances at the youth shelter and at work.

Was Lin's brother, Jian, ever really here? I figure there's no harm in checking for clues. No idea what to look for, but I start with the closet in Ben's room. Apart from the old hoodies and shirts and jeans I've hung up in there, the clothes are all expensive brands. Not the kind of thing street kids own.

There are six pairs of cool sneakers on a shelf at the back that I hadn't noticed before. Wow! Who has shoes like that and hides them in a closet? They're not in mint condition, like Ben is saving them as collector's items or anything. He's definitely worn them all. But maybe he was worried about them being stolen at school? Whatever. Like the clothes, those shoes aren't ones a street kid could afford.

Next I go through the bathroom cupboards and drawers. Which is ridiculous, because what am I going to find? A toothbrush with Jian's name on it? Or a bus pass or something with photo ID? There's nothing but the sample-size toiletries that look like they came from a fancy hotel. Not that I've ever stayed at one, but people who saved them on their travels used to drop them off at the youth shelter.

The body wash and shampoo are mostly used up now, but they were new when I moved in. Which proves exactly nothing. If Jian had been living here, Reba's cleaning service would have replaced those things when he disappeared. Or ran away or whatever he did.

I search around the rest of the house, including snooping in Reba's office. But all I find is evidence that Ben lives here. And that he's good-looking and also good at everything. There are photos of him surfing and skiing, running on the soccer field and playing the grand piano in the living room. There's his grad photo and one of him with his arm around a beautiful girl.

And then there's one of him on a boat. He's wearing sunglasses and holding a beer, laughing into the camera. I can just see the name of the boat in the background. It's called *Tax Haven Maven*.

So for sure Reba has a boat. But I can't find anything in her house that answers my questions. Was Lin's brother ever here? And if he was, where has he gone?

I keep seeing Lin's face and how upset she was. I want to believe her. And if her brother really is gone, I want to help her. But first I need to know she's not a scammer. Or just plain crazy.

The best thing to do is ask Reba. See what she has to say. That night at dinner, as we're eating the herb-roasted pork tenderloin with mushroom-cornbread stuffing I made, I go for it. "Living here has really saved my life. So I was wondering, how many kids have you helped?"

"Helped?" She takes a drink of wine. "In what way?"

"You know, taken in, like me. Given them a job and a place to stay until they got back on their feet. You said something like, 'Helping kids in need is the least I can do.'" I dig into my dinner, which is excellent, if I do say so myself.

"Oh, of course. Sorry—I was thinking about work. I have a high-stakes case on right now, and it's taking all my focus." She drinks some more wine. "Actually," she says, with a little laugh, "you're the first."

Wait. What? "Really? Nobody else? Because you said you'd had someone, but he got a job and moved out."

"Oh, that was my nephew from Ontario, not a street kid." She finishes her wine and pours herself another glass. I've noticed she drinks quite a lot. Like, a whole bottle, every night.

I guess her rule about no substance abuse of any kind only applies to kids, not to her. But it's her house, her rule. Not up to me to judge.

Still, I am a bit suspicious of her now. "You made it sound like you'd taken in other kids. Why did you do that?"

"I didn't want to scare you off. I wanted to help you, because I remembered you from Cedarvale, but I wasn't sure you'd trust me."

She's right about that. I feel like she tricked me into coming here. "Yeah, I would have said no if I'd known I was the first kid you've let live here." Well, probably. But maybe not. I didn't exactly have any other options.

"I apologize for that, Kipp. I hope you can forgive me."

"It's okay. I'm not worried. I was just curious, you know?"

"Yes, of course. I should have been straight with you." She picks up her fork and finishes off her dinner. "This stuffing is delicious, by the way."

Is she changing the subject? "Thanks. It's my own recipe. But just to be clear, you've never had a guy called Jian living here?"

"Jian?" She stands and begins clearing our plates. "No. Never heard of anyone called Jian. Lovely name though." She carries the dishes to the counter and says, with her back to me, "Why do you ask?"

I almost tell her about Lin coming by looking for him. But something stops me. I don't know what Lin's deal is, but I'm kind of mad at Reba for lying to me. And there is something off about her reaction to my questions. I don't feel like sharing anything with her right now.

Just in case Lin is right.

But honestly? I don't know who or what to believe.

Chapter Seven

Should I get in touch with Lin and tell her I couldn't find any evidence of Jian living here? And that Reba says she's never heard of him? But Lin didn't give me her phone number.

I google her parents' bakery. Happy Cookies is way on the other side of the city. It would take an hour or so on the bus to get there. I guess I could phone her at work, but it's not news she'll be happy to hear.

And I'm still not sure about her story, especially now that Reba denies it.

Why would I doubt Reba and believe what some random girl says? Just because Lin's pretty and I liked her doesn't mean she's not lying. Reba's been so good to me. Well, except for tricking me into coming here. But it's a great job and a great place to live.

I can't decide what to do. All I know is, something's not right.

And then, a couple of days later, Lin comes by again. I'm in the driveway, washing Reba's Mazda 6. Yeah, her second car. Reba drives this one on weekends, not to work. She backed it out of her garage before she left this morning, since I don't have a license. I've got cloths, polish and a car vac ready to finish the job.

I don't know why Reba didn't just take the car to a detailing shop. She could afford it, and they'd do a way better job than I can. But it's making work for me at fifteen dollars an hour—which is probably the reason she didn't, now that I think of it. It's really nice of her to help me earn money, so I'm on it.

My sneakers are soaked, and my jeans and hoodie are kind of wet too. Washing Reba's car got me remembering my uncle and how he used to make me wash and polish his truck when it was all muddy from him driving on back roads. His truck was his baby, and he'd stand there drinking a beer and criticizing me, telling me how I was doing everything wrong. It made me so mad I once turned the hose on too hard, lost hold and got soaked.

"Hey, Lin," I say when I see her. "Find your brother yet?"

She's even prettier than I remember. Today she has her hair in one of those topknot things, and it suits her face. "No, I was hoping you'd found him."

"Yeah, about that. I looked, but there's no proof he was ever in the house. So then I asked Reba, and guess what? She said he never lived here. She's never even heard of him."

Lin's mouth drops open. "What? She actually said that?"

"She did."

"She's lying."

"Why would she lie?" I pick up a cloth and start drying the car. "I mean, Reba's a lawyer and all. She's a professional, respectable person."

"And I'm not? Because I'm a kid and I work in a bakery? Because I'm not some rich lady letting you live in her house?"

"Look, I don't know why, but I think you're making it up about your brother."

"Oh my god, I'm not! I swear I'm not. I'm just so worried about him." Lin bursts into tears. She wipes at her eyes with her hands, smearing her makeup. "I think she did something to him, and that's why she's lying! She's covering her tracks!"

"C'mon, don't be so dramatic. He probably just told you he was living here so you wouldn't worry about him. So you'd think he was doing okay."

"But why would he have given me this address? And I saw him here. Twice. I visited him when she was out at work."

"Really?" News to me. "Why didn't you tell me that before?"

"Didn't get a chance. And I thought you'd find him."

"Okay, prove it. Tell me about the inside of the house."

And she does. She describes everything in detail. Even down to the photos everywhere of Reba's son, Ben, and his collection of fancy sneakers. "Now do you believe me?"

Maybe?

But maybe not so fast. "You could know all that from breaking in."

Lin crosses her arms and actually stamps her foot. "You have to believe me. I never broke in! I visited Jian here."

"Okay, whatever. But your brother's definitely not here now."

"No, because she took him out on her boat and he never came back."

"So, like, she threw him overboard or something? If you're so worried, why don't you ask your parents for help?"

"No point. They kicked him out when he quit working in the bakery and started doing drugs. They don't care what happens to him. He's dishonored them."

Hmm. "Did Jian tell you that Reba has a rule about no drugs?"

"Yeah. He didn't like it, but he wanted to stay here, so he followed it."

"Right." I bet he didn't. But she looks so devastated, I can't tell her that. "Go to the cops then. File a missing-person report."

"Seriously?" She looks at me like I've got two heads. "The cops don't care about street kids. You should know that."

Yeah, I do. Of course I do. "Okay, tell you what. Give me your number, and I'll call if I find out anything."

I pull out my phone. She takes it and shrieks, "Oh my god! That's the phone she gave Jian!"

"Wait. What?"

"When he lived here. She gave him this phone so she could text him about his jobs and stuff."

My stomach drops. "Are you sure? I thought you said his phone was out of service."

"Well, of course she'd change the number. But that was Jian's phone! I recognize the case."

The phone has a shiny black case with gold lettering that says *Newton & Rabinovitch*. That's the name of Reba's law firm. My heart pounds.

"Even if it is, I'm sure there's a good explanation."

"Don't kid yourself," Lin says. "You're her next victim."

Chapter Eight

What the hell just happened?

Lin says I've got the phone Reba gave Jian. What's going on?

I'm starting to believe Lin and suspect Reba, that's what.

After I finish detailing Reba's car, I go downstairs to Ben's room and google Reba. Guess I should have done that before I came to live here.

I find her firm's website, which has stuff about the services they provide and the lawyers who work there. Reba's bio lists where she went to school, cases she's worked on, awards she's won and bits about her community service. It mentions she was a volunteer at Cedarvale Youth Shelter.

Her profile picture must be about twenty years out of date though. She looks way older now. From our many dinner conversations, I know she feels really pressured by her work. Her clients are all high-profile and demanding. They don't want to pay a penny more in tax than they need to. They don't want to be charged with tax evasion. And they expect her to advise and protect them.

There's nothing on her firm's website that would make me suspicious. I even check out a website where people can rate lawyers, and she's highly ranked. So why would someone like Reba lie about Jian?

Next I click on her Facebook page. And that's where I find what I'm looking for. Her most recent post, from over six months ago, almost makes me throw up. It's about her son, Ben.

Turns out, he's not away at school. He dropped out of college. He's been missing for over a year.

I sit there staring at his high-school grad photo. Reba's post says, *Before things went wrong.* I scroll down through her earlier posts. After Ben left school he came home, but she kicked him out because he was into drugs. She cut off his funds, so he became a dealer. He ended up an addict, living on the street.

She doesn't know where he is. She's so sorry about losing touch and wants to find him, get him help. She begs anyone with any info at all to contact her.

I google Ben, but there's nothing recent. Only old stuff, mostly about sports.

Holy crap!

This is unbelievable! Reba lied about her son! Just like she lied about Jian.

What have I gotten myself into?

I want to punch something. But the last time I did that, I got fired.

So maybe I'll just get drunk or high. Or both. I thought I was past all that, but of course you never really are.

Reba's got beer and wine in the fridge and a fully stocked bar. And I bet there's Xanax or Ativan in her bathroom cabinet too.

She'd never notice anything missing. But then again, with her one rule, she might. She asks me every day if I'm clean. And I bet she knows the signs.

Guess I know where her rule comes from now though. Well, who cares about her stupid rule? She's a liar, and she tricked me into living here.

I race upstairs.

Back when I lived with my uncle in Helston Bay, I tried lots of stuff, just to see what it was like. I wasn't dependent on alcohol or drugs. But Fern's death broke me. Before I got help through Cedarvale, I was in bad shape.

Do I really want to make that kind of choice again? Avoid my problems with substance abuse?

Yup, I do.

I've got a beer in my hand, ready to open, when I see Fern's face in my mind. Hear her voice. She would be so mad at me for giving in. For taking the easy road. For not facing up to my situation and trying to find a better way to deal with this.

Fern would want me to help Lin. And if Reba kicks me out, how will I help Lin find out where Jian is?

Getting drunk will feel good at first. But I'll be sorry later. And it won't solve anything.

I know that. I totally know that. I learned the hard way.

I put the beer back, grab a soda and start making dinner.

Cooking always grounds me. Paying attention to the steps in a recipe gives me a focus. And that helps me control my emotions. Making a good meal is a positive thing. It will keep me on track for honoring Fern's memory by making something of my life.

And while I'm eating dinner with Reba, I'll try to get some answers.

Reba comes home from work just as I finish making dinner. Tonight it's Moroccan chicken with couscous.

"Dinner smells delicious," she says as she pours herself some wine.

I want a drink so much I can't look at the bottle. I concentrate on dishing up our plates. "Thanks. I know you like spicy food, and I've been wanting to try this recipe."

"Happy to be your taste tester." She takes a long drink of wine, then a bite of chicken. "Oh, Kipp, this is so good."

I eat some too, and she's right. It's fantastic. "Glad you like it. How was work?"

"Brutal." She finishes off her wine and pours another glass, as usual. "But I don't want to talk about it. Can't talk about it, actually. How was your day?"

Also brutal. I found out that Ben's not away at school. I'm confused and scared. "I got your Mazda all washed up. Hope it's okay."

"Yes, thanks. It looked great when I put it back in the garage." She sets down her fork and tilts her head at me. "And you're following my rule?"

"Yup. And you don't have to ask me every single day."

"You sound a bit defensive. Anything you want to tell me?"

I am not going to mention how tempted I was earlier. "No. You can trust me."

She doesn't answer. We eat in silence for a few minutes, and then I get my nerve up and say, "Oh, hey, I was wondering about your son."

"Ben? What about him?"

"Well, I know you said he probably won't be home over the holidays, but I'd really like to meet him sometime. I mean, judging from all the pictures of him, he seems like a great guy."

Reba coughs and flails her hands about like she's choking.

"You okay?" I jump up to get her a glass of water, knocking over my chair.

She gulps some water and says, "Sorry, that bit went down the wrong way. I'm fine." She sips some more while I pick up my chair.

"How's Ben doing at college anyway?" Now my words come out too fast and sound fake. "What's he studying?"

Reba tries to make eye contact. Does she suspect me? I can't look at her, or I'll give myself away. She serves herself more chicken from the dish on the table. "Ben's at med school, doing brilliantly. And it's his final year, so he'll be home next summer to do a residency here. You can meet him then."

"Cool! Can't wait." And I can't help snickering about catching her in a lie, which morphs into nervous laughter.

"Kipp!" Reba's voice is stern. "Are you high?"

"No. Promise." How can I explain why I'm acting goofy? This is so messed up. Did she really think I'd never find out the truth?

But I can't let on that I know about Ben, or she'll kick me out. And I need to stay here to find out where Jian is. What she's done to him.

"You'd better not be. Because I *will* find out."

"Understood."

"Oh, and by the way," she says, her voice pleasant again, "how would you like to go for a boat ride on the weekend?"

OMG! No effing way! "Um, a boat ride? Like, where exactly?"

"I've got a cabin cruiser down at West Seaside Marina. We could take a run up to Salish Island. The forecast is clear, and it might be the last nice weather we have until spring. I don't really take the boat out in the winter."

I can't speak.

Salish Island is where she was taking Jian.

And going out on her boat is the last thing on earth I want to do.

I'm not sure I can make myself go with her. It's too terrifying.

But then I think of Fern and Lin and Jian. Maybe I can find out what happened. "Sure," I say. "Sounds good."

Chapter Nine

For the next three days I'm scared to death. Did I really agree to go out on Reba's boat? The thought of it makes my stomach churn. But I force myself to act excited so she won't suspect anything.

It's really hard to keep from taking a drink. But I need a clear head. I need Reba to trust me so I can find out about Jian.

And I also need backup. Lin should know where I've gone, in case I disappear. Like Jian did.

The trip to Salish Island is planned for Sunday. So on Saturday I make the bus trip across the city to Happy Cookies, the bakery owned by Lin's parents. I know I could just call Lin, now that I have her number. But I really want to see her.

I still love and miss Fern. She'll always be in my heart. But I can't live in the past. Fern will stay seventeen forever, but I have to grow up and get on with my life. At some time or other, I'm going to meet another girl I'm attracted to. Okay, I already have. And it's worth a long, boring bus trip to visit her.

Happy Cookies is on a street that used to be a bit rough. But now it's gone all trendy. The bakery is super busy. I almost can't get in the door. There are families and hipsters and business types and seniors waiting to be served.

I can see Lin behind the counter, so I get in line and look around. They sure have a lot of different kinds of cookies. And a whole glass case of those decorated cookies in every shape—animals, fish, flowers, stars, hearts and smiley faces. Everything looks great.

I have lots of time to read all the prices and learn that the bakery specializes in custom cookies for special occasions. Like for birthdays, weddings, baby showers, anniversaries or whatever. Anything you want, they can make it for you. With forty-eight hours' notice and payment in advance.

Lin's wearing a pink apron that says *Happy Cookies Make Happy Days* in red lettering. On her head is a funny little pink hat with red trim that I think is supposed to look like some kind of flower cookie. She's working fast to serve all the customers. She bags or boxes their orders without missing a beat, like she's done it all her life. Which maybe she has.

But when she sees me next in line, she messes up. She gives the customer before me a dozen oatmeal-cranberry cookies instead of chocolate chip. Once she's fixed that order, she turns and calls toward the back, "Mom! I need to take a break."

She pulls off her plastic gloves as a woman who looks a lot like Lin comes out to mind the counter. The woman glares at me like I might be an alien. "Five minutes," she says. "I've got orders to finish."

Lin brings me into a back room where a man is working on a laptop. "Dad, this is Kipp."

Her dad shuts the computer, stands and gives me the once-over.

"Hello, Mr. Cheng." I hold out my hand to shake his.

He doesn't take it. Lin says quickly, "Kipp's working at that lady's house where Jian was. Remember I told you about Jian staying there?"

"Jian?" Mr. Cheng says. "I don't know any Jian."

"Dad, please. Kipp might have news." Lin touches my arm. "Do you? Did you find out anything?"

Before I can answer, Mr. Cheng says, "Back to work, Lin."

"But Dad—"

"Back to work."

Lin grabs a coat from a hook on the wall and goes outside instead. I follow, and we talk in the alley behind the bakery. "Your parents are really strict, eh?"

"Yeah. They're so worried I'll end up like Jian. That I'll get into drugs or prostitution and not go to college. Like I've ever given them any reason to think that. But tell me what you've found out."

I talk as fast as I can. Now I kind of wish I'd phoned her, because I don't want to get Lin in trouble. She's as shocked as I was about Ben being missing, not away at school. And she's thrilled about Reba wanting to take me to Salish Island.

"You're going, right?" she says. "I know she's psycho, but you have to go."

I wish I could just say no. But I like Lin too much already. "Yeah, I'll go. I kind of don't like boats though."

"Oh, you get seasick?"

"Something like that." I'm not ready to tell her about my mom and that canoe tipping over and me almost drowning. "I'll be okay."

Her face lights up with a smile. "Thanks so much. I really appreciate it. It's the first time I've had hope in months." Her smile fades, and her face goes serious. "Okay, I better get back in there. Good luck, and keep in touch."

"I will." And that's for my sake as much as hers. Because what if Jian's dead or something? What if I need to be rescued? I might have to call Lin for help. "I'll let you know right away if I have news."

"Thanks again." She gives me a hug. My heart skips a beat. And then it skips another when she adds, "Be careful. That woman is dangerous."

Chapter Ten

That night I can't sleep. I've changed my mind. I'm not going out on a boat! Especially not with a crazy person!

I'm just not that brave.

I have a strong urge to run, like I did after Fern died. It was a mistake coming to live at Reba's. I should have gone back to Cedarvale.

Well, it's not too late. I can still do that.

But what about Jian? I want to help Lin find her brother. I can't chicken out and disappoint her.

I have to do this. Even if I die of fear.

Morning comes way too soon.

Before we leave, I check that my phone is fully charged. The plan is for me to keep in close contact with Lin. I'll feel safer if she knows where I am, and she'll be less worried if I give her updates.

I text her when we set out. She texts back wishing me good luck.

I'm going to need it.

Except for that time I almost drowned, the only boat I've ever been on was the ferry to Vancouver when I left Helston Bay. But the ferry is a huge boat—it holds four hundred cars or something. Not nearly as scary as going out on the ocean in Reba's boat will be.

Besides being scared of boats, I can't actually swim. I never took lessons. The closest public pool when I was a kid was almost an hour from Helston Bay. My uncle refused to sign me up and drive me there.

He figured I should learn the way he did, from other kids. At Dogwood Lake, where I almost drowned.

I did go to Dogwood Lake a lot. But all I ever did there was horse around in the shallow water. Once I made it out to the raft with the help of a boogie board, but I was terrified the whole time. When kids jumped off the dock, I lay on my towel in the sun. When kids rented canoes or kayaks or stand-up paddleboards, I never took a ride. I couldn't even watch. I got called a wimp, and worse, but I didn't care.

At least I get to ride to West Seaside Marina in Reba's Mazda. Which distracts me from obsessing about tides and currents and wind and waves and suddenly changing weather.

I text Lin again when we get there: **So far, so good.**

Before we'd left the house, Reba called the marina and asked them to have her boat fueled up, and I loaded her car with boxes of dried food and bottled water. When we've parked, she shows me where to get a wheelbarrow to cart the boxes down to her boat. She has a code to open the gates onto the dock.

Man, there's a lot of boats moored here. Who owns all these? Rich people, I guess. All of them not going out today. All of them safe at home. Where I wish I was.

It's a relief to see that the *Tax Haven Maven* is way bigger than I expected. And I have to admit it's a beauty, white with black trim and a sleek design. But even though it's tied to the dock, it rocks when I step on board with one of the boxes. And then again when I step off for another.

Oh, jeez. I hate this so much.

Reba points to the motor at the back. "Two hundred horsepower," she says, like I'll know what that means. But it looks impressive and sounds fast.

She boards and goes to check whatever she has to check before we leave. After she's started the engine, she comes back and tells me to untie the lines.

As I do, the boat swings away from the dock.

"Jump aboard," Reba shouts.

I scramble and almost don't make it. I land like a klutz, fall onto the deck, swear and stumble trying to get up.

Reba gives me a hand. "Are you on something? What did you take?"

"No, nothing. Honest. I've just never been on a boat like this before." My stomach is queasy already. "I'm kind of nervous. Do you have life jackets?"

"Of course." She finds me one, and I put it on and do it up. Tight.

The rest of the boat is amazing. It has beds and a kitchen and everything. It's all dark woodwork, with stainless-steel trim, and navy-blue upholstery. I take a photo and text it to Lin. She sends me a thumbs-up.

Reba points out the bathroom, which she calls the head, then says, "Come up to the helm." I follow her and then, to calm my nerves, focus on watching her drive. She looks all around, puts the boat in reverse and steers expertly out of the slip. The motor thrums, and we move slowly into the harbor.

When we clear the No Wake zone, Reba opens up the throttle, and we gain speed. The water sparkles blue and green in the sun, and there's fresh snow on the mountain peaks. People in other boats smile and wave as we pass.

The water is calm, and it's a pretty smooth ride. I feel myself start to relax. Maybe I'll be okay after all.

But then we round a point and leave the protected harbor behind.

The bow lifts as we hit a wave, then smacks back down. As Reba steers into the open sea, the wind picks up, and the water grows choppy. Now the engine roars, and with every wave we hit, water sprays up over the bow.

Suddenly Reba's boat seems tiny.

I check that my life jacket is still done up tightly and ask, "What are the safety features of this boat?" That one time I rode on the ferry, they made an announcement about what to do in case of emergency. Where the life boats were and stuff like that. "What if we capsize?"

"We won't."

God, I hope not. Just last year a whale-watching boat got hit by a rogue wave, and some tourists were swept away and never found. And the year before that, a fishing boat got swamped near Helston Bay, and everybody on board drowned.

"But it's the open ocean," I say. "A force of nature. Unpredictable."

"Calm down, Kipp. I have a marine radio, horn, flares, flags and flashlights."

"Oh." Somehow that's not as reassuring as I'd like.

"Don't worry. We'd be rescued." She doesn't look at me, though, just grips the wheel and stares out through the windshield at the rough water.

Thank God I can see Salish Island coming up fast. I can't wait to get off this thing and feel land under my feet.

But Reba doesn't slow down. She doesn't steer us to the dock. She drives right on past.

"Hey!" I shout over the roar of the engine and wind and waves. "Where are we going?"

Chapter Eleven

Salish Island shrinks smaller and smaller as we leave it behind. The waves grow bigger and bigger. Water sprays up and over the boat and onto the deck as we hit them.

Smack, slosh. Smack, slosh. Smack, slosh.

Reba doesn't answer my question about where we're going.

I try to text Lin, but there's no reception.

I think I'm gonna throw up.

Just in time, another island appears. It looks like nothing other than harsh rocks and dense forest, but Reba steers toward it. We circle to the east side, where the water is calmer. Now I can see an old wooden dock and some boarded-up fishing shacks on a rocky point.

There's a weathered sign that says *Bracken Island. Rentals available.* There's a phone number too, but the sign is so faded I can't read it.

Reba cuts the engine and brings us parallel to the dock. Bumpers on the side of the boat keep us from hitting too hard. She tells me to jump out and tie up.

I leap off the boat like my life depends on it. The rickety dock rocks under me. It's wet and slippery, and I'm shaking so hard I can hardly tie the lines. But I'm stoked to be off the boat. Don't know how I'm going to make myself get back on when we leave.

"Okay, let's unload."

"Unload?"

"Can you give me a hand, please?" Reba starts hefting boxes of supplies onto the dock.

"Those aren't for your boat?"

"No."

I grab a box. "Where should I take this?"

"Up there." Reba points to the one shack on the rocky point that isn't boarded up. "My brother's place," she says. "Ben loves to come here when he's home. Used to spend a couple of weeks here every summer."

There's no wheelbarrow to cart the boxes. It's going to be a slog to lug everything up to that shack. My bulky life jacket makes it hard to work, so I take it off and toss it back into the boat. I pull my hood up over my head to keep my ears warm.

The air is cold and damp, and I wish I'd worn a jacket over my hoodie. And a warm wool cap and gloves like Reba has. She did tell me to dress in layers, but I didn't know we were coming way up here. I thought we were only going to Salish Island, where we'd get a hot lunch in a café.

Moving the boxes is hard work. And treacherous. There are places where the boards of the dock are loose and broken. Everything is slippery and covered with moss. My bare hands are freezing.

When we've finally struggled up to the shack with most of the boxes, Reba says, "Let's take a break. We can get the rest later."

"Okay, sure. But I have a question. Why did you say we were going to Salish Island?"

Reba gives a little laugh. "Oh, I thought it would sound more fun."

"And you didn't think I'd come if you told me where we were really going?"

"Well, everyone wants to go to Salish Island."

"Yeah, because it's got a store and a café and stuff. People actually live there."

"People live here too."

"But not in the winter. So why are we bringing all this stuff? I thought it was for stocking your boat."

Reba doesn't answer, just opens the door of the shack. It's dark and cold and smells musty inside. There's no hydro, just a camp stove, some lanterns and a cot with a sleeping bag. But it's obvious someone has been living here. The place is littered with empty soda cans and water bottles and packaging from dried food.

All the things we've got in the boxes.

I get a sick feeling. A different sick feeling than I had on the boat.

"Is Jian here?" I ask. "Is this where you came when you told him you were taking him to Salish Island?"

Reba gasps. "How do you know that?"

"Because his sister came by your house looking for him. She's crazy worried. Remember I asked you about him? And you said you'd never heard of him?"

Reba pulls off her gloves and stuffs them into the pocket of her windbreaker. "He broke my rule. He was doing drugs at my house."

"And so you, like, left him alone here for two whole weeks? In November?"

Reba shrugs. "He had to get clean."

Wow. That's insane. Who leaves a kid stranded on a remote, deserted island?

Someone who is in denial about her own son, that's who. I'm tempted to confront Reba about Ben—tell her I found out he's not away at school. But I'm alone here with her. Who knows how she'd react or what she might do?

I need to concentrate on finding Jian. I look all around, like he might be hiding somewhere. Except the shack is just one room, and there's nowhere to hide. "Where's Jian?"

"Don't know. Out in the woods maybe?"

I'm shocked at how unconcerned she is. "Don't you think we should look for him? Take him back with us?"

"Of course. You go ahead and try to find him. I'll start on those other boxes, then come back and help."

She heads down to the dock. I follow the boardwalk lined with shacks right to the end, where it turns into a path leading up over the rocky point or off into the forest. "Jian!" I yell. "Jian!" I can't wait to let Lin know I've found him. That he's here, and we're bringing him home.

And then I hear the *Tax Haven Maven* starting up. I turn and see Reba driving away.

Holy shit!

She's left me stranded here too!

Chapter Twelve

I rush back down to the dock, trying not to fall on the slippery boardwalk. Waving madly, I yell, "Stop! Reba, please stop! Come back for me!"

But of course she can't hear me. And she wouldn't return anyway. She knows I'm not on board. Leaving me on Bracken Island was her plan all along.

I've been so stupid. I should have known when she didn't actually answer my question about why she didn't tell me we were coming here. Or when she told me she'd left Jian here to get clean. I should have realized she didn't believe me all the times I told her I wasn't doing drugs. I should have figured it out when we brought all those supplies up to the shack instead of unpacking them on her boat.

But I'd been too distracted by wanting to find Jian. I'd been so excited that I had news for Lin. All I could think about was how happy she'd be.

I stand there like an idiot, watching the *Tax Haven Maven* speed off until it's so far away it looks like a toy boat. And then it finally disappears. It's gone. Just freakin' gone.

I try again to text Lin, but there's no service. Great. Will Reba ever come back? Or am I stranded here all winter, until people start going out fishing regularly again? Because there's not nearly enough food and water for that.

I tell myself not to panic. Jian didn't have a phone with him. But I do. There has to be someplace on

Bracken Island with reception. And I need to find it. Fast.

I hurry back up to the shack and try my phone, but still no luck. I follow the boardwalk again, farther and farther along, but no reception bars. Crap! At the end, instead of taking the path into the forest, I go the other way. Head toward what looks like the highest point on the island.

The rocks here are rugged and bare except for a few stunted fir trees, their branches windblown into a slanted shape. As I start climbing, I find out why. The wind is wild, and I have to grab hold of branches and exposed roots to keep from being blown away.

When I finally make it to the top, I'm on a cliff above the sea. I try my phone again, holding it way up in the air. Still nothing. Not good. So not good. Because if there's no reception here, I'm not likely to find it anywhere else. And now I have to scramble all the way back down, which will be harder than getting up was.

My hands are already scraped raw from the branches and rocks. I tuck them into my hoodie pocket, trying to warm them. Maybe there's another way back if I try the other side. I go right to the edge of the cliff to have a look.

Jeez, it's a long way down.

And oh my god! There's a body lying on the beach below.

A body that's not moving. A body with one leg at an odd angle.

It has to be Jian. Did he fall from this cliff or what?

I don't stop to think. I just scramble down the far side of the cliff, which is less steep. It's not easy, but I have to get to him.

"Jian!" I call. "Are you okay?"

He doesn't answer. Is he unconscious or something?

I near the beach. The rocks here are covered with barnacles that cut my hands even more. I have to creep along, because there's also a lot of gooey, green seaweed. The air smells like salt and dead fish.

Finally I make it to Jian, who is lying in a heap on his side. He looks pretty bad, all dirty and scrawny. "Hey, man, can you hear me?"

He lets out a moan. And then, "Help me. Please help me."

"It's okay. I'll get you out of here." I have no idea how though. From the look of that leg, he won't be able to climb up the rocks. And we're in a little cove. There's no other exit.

"I'm a friend of Lin's. She sent me to find you."

Jian nods his head and winces with pain.

"What happened?" I ask. "You fell down the cliff?"

Jian groans. "Heard a boat. Tried to signal for help."

I see there's a grubby white T-shirt lying beside him. "You climbed up to the top and were using that as a flag?"

"Almost every day," he says. "Nobody ever sees me."

"You've been trying to be rescued for two weeks? Since Reba left you here?"

Jian nods, and his eyes close.

"Hey." I shake his shoulder, but he's passed out.

And then I realize that he's below the tide line.

It looks like the tide is still going out, but it's only a matter of time until it comes in again. Even if I can't get Jian up the cliff, I have to get him higher up the beach.

I'm not sure I should move him though. Won't that make his injuries worse? I try my phone again, just in case. But nothing.

I scan the horizon, hoping to see a boat nearby. More nothing. There's a freighter way out and a tugboat pulling a log boom. But neither are anywhere near close enough to see us. And if Jian's been waving his flag every day with no one noticing, what hope do I have now?

Chapter Thirteen

We're on a pebble beach in a narrow cove, alone with the greedy gulls pecking for sea creatures exposed by the low tide. A line of foam marks the high-tide line, littered with bunches of eelgrass and kelp. Above that lie heaps of driftwood logs that have been thrown up by storm waves, and beyond is the rocky cliff.

It's going to start getting dark in a couple of hours. The tide's going to change. Jian's injured and probably dehydrated and starving. We're both shivering in the cold, damp air.

I really need to figure something out.

If only I was still wearing my life jacket. I could put it on Jian so he'd float when the tide came in, and I could pull him to safety. If only I'd thought of bringing some food and water with me. If only a lot of things, none of which are going to help me now.

At least Lin knows I went out on Reba's boat. When she doesn't hear from me by late afternoon, she'll send help. But she thinks we went to Salish Island. By the time anybody looks for me there, it will be too late. Jian and I will both be dead of exposure.

And if anyone tries to contact Reba, will she answer her door or her phone? Because she knows now that Lin came by looking for Jian. I wish I hadn't given her a heads-up that Lin was onto her.

I wish I knew what to do.

I think back to what Reba said she had on her boat to signal for help. A marine radio, a horn, flares, flags and flashlights. We don't have the first three. And Jian's T-shirt flag hasn't worked so far.

But I do have a phone with an almost fully charged battery. And it has a flashlight!

I saw this old movie once where a guy on a boat used Morse code to send an SOS signal with a flashlight. I just can't remember what the sequence of flashes is supposed to be. Three long and three short, or the other way around? Or maybe short first and then long? Or something else?

"Do you know Morse code?" I ask Jian. But his eyes are still closed.

I stare out at the horizon, trying to remember how you do it. But I can't. All I know for sure is that it's starting to drizzle and the tide is definitely coming in.

Waves that were lapping at the shore are now heaving and breaking. The beach pebbles roll about and make a clattering sound when the ocean sucks back.

Should I leave Jian and go get the sleeping bag and some food and water? Could I carry them down the cliff? What if I fall and get hurt too? What if a rogue wave hits the beach and swamps Jian?

I take off my hoodie and use it to cover him, trying to stop his shivering. I start flashing my light. On, off. On, off. On, off. I'm useless at it. Even if I knew the right way to do SOS, I'm so scared and shivery myself that I can't keep track. On, off. On, off. On, off.

It's pointless anyway. If I can't see any boats out there, how is anybody going to see my light? I don't want to waste the battery, so I'll wait until there's something to send a signal to.

Like maybe somebody out fishing. But I didn't see any small fishing boats all the way here. And there was nobody at the shacks.

I keep one eye on the horizon and the other on the tide. Luckily Jian's feet are closer to the water than his head is. But the waves will soon be washing over his sneakers.

The seagulls lift off, circle and shriek. Their cries sound like *help, help, help*. Or maybe *die, die, die*. Either way, it's like they know we're doomed.

I stand and try to haul Jian up the beach a bit. But he's a dead weight. And he jerks awake at the pain. "Stop!" he moans. "Effing hurts, man!"

"Sorry." I don't want to tell him about the tide. "Have you ever seen any boats closer in than the freighters?" I ask.

"Fishing boats," he says. "Big commercial ones. Most days."

Of course. I used to see them all the time in Helston Bay. Out at dawn, home at dusk. "But they never noticed your flag?"

"Nope." His eyes close again.

I wonder if there's a commercial dock on Salish Island. If there is, the boats would go in and out from there. And if we're lucky, some will be passing by here in the next while.

The light fades and the tide flows in. I'm soaked

with drizzle, and my teeth are chattering. My hands are so numb I almost can't hold my phone anymore. Plus I can't keep it dry.

On, off. On, off. On, off.

It feels like forever before I see a big gray fishing boat coming.

On, off. On, off. On, off.

No response. The boat keeps going.

Then there's another. It's smaller and is closer to Bracken Island. I can even see the crew on deck.

I work my flashlight again.

On, off. On, off. On, off.

Please. Please. Please.

Jian has stopped shivering, which I think is a sign of hypothermia. I'm feeling disoriented and like I might pass out. I can't keep going much longer.

And then the boat is coming in even closer. They're lowering a dinghy. Somebody's rowing it to shore.

Somebody's landing it on the beach. Asking questions, checking Jian. Calling the coast guard because they don't want to move him.

They cover us both with shiny silver survival blankets.

I try to explain what happened, but I don't make a lot of sense. I'm crying and rambling about Reba and drugs, and they must think I'm on something.

"Hang in there," somebody says. "Chopper's coming."

Soon there's noise and wind worse than a hurricane above us.

Bright lights shine, and voices yell, "Down here, down here!"

Paramedics rappel down the cliff, get Jian onto a backboard and place an oxygen mask over his face.

Someone lifts and carries me.

Chapter Fourteen

Next thing I know, I'm in a hospital with an IV line stuck in my hand. What the hell?

There's a nurse in blue scrubs beside my bed, making notes on a chart. When he sees I'm awake, he says, "Hypothermia. We'll keep you in overnight to monitor your vitals, but you should be fine."

It all comes back to me then. Reba leaving me stranded on Bracken Island, finding Jian on the beach, trying for hours to get help, the fishing boat coming and calling the coast guard, the helicopter ride here. "What about Jian?" I ask. "Is he okay?"

"Your friend's in surgery for a badly broken leg." The nurse places the chart in a holder by the door. "He didn't have any ID on him, but we had to go ahead. Can you let his family know?" He hands me my phone, which was on the table beside me.

"Where have you been?" Lin wants to know when I reach her the next day. "I've been going nuts. I called the cops when I didn't hear from you and told them where Reba lives, but they didn't do anything."

"There was a cop here," I tell her. "She met us when search and rescue brought us in last night. She's coming back later to talk to me."

"I'll be there too. I'm on my way."

Next I call Reba. She doesn't answer, but I didn't think she would. I leave her a long pissed-off message telling her what happened. Telling her the cops want to talk to her and so do I, and she'd better get down here.

I'm surprised when she actually shows up. She rushes in looking like she had a rough night too. Her makeup is smeared, and her hair's a mess. Instead of her usual dark business suit, she's wearing faded jeans and a baggy old sweater.

"Oh, Kipp. I am so, so sorry," she says, bursting into tears. "I don't know what I was thinking. I should never have left you there, or Jian either. But he was doing drugs, and I thought you were too, and I so wanted to help you stop."

"Yeah, well, you almost killed us."

"Sorry, sorry, sorry." Sob, sob, sob.

"Thanks, but sorry is not enough."

"I know, I know." Boo, hoo, hoo.

"And I know about Ben," I tell her. "I saw your Facebook posts. He's not away at school. He's been missing for a year."

She gulps in air and cries harder. When she gets herself under control a bit, she says, "Everybody told me I had to let him hit rock bottom, but that didn't work. He just disappeared. He could be dead for all I know. All I wanted to do was make up for kicking him out. He went to Bracken Island twice to get clean, and it worked. Until it didn't."

She starts sobbing again.

"Is that why you were volunteering at Cedarvale? To try to find him?"

She nods and grabs a tissue from the box beside my bed. She wipes her eyes and blows her nose. "I kept hoping he'd show up or somebody who would know where he was. The last time I saw him was in the park where I met you that day. I go there all the time looking for him." She takes another tissue and clutches it in her hand. "I was in denial and couldn't face telling you the truth. And then it was too late. Can you ever forgive me?"

I'm not sure, but I don't have to answer because the cop from last night comes into the room. "Reba Newton? I have some questions for you."

But before she can ask them, Reba admits to everything. "I know I need help," she adds. "I had a breakdown when my son went missing, and I stayed at Westaway Center for a month. I know I've been acting crazy and delusional, and I think I need to go back there."

"We're going to have more questions, and Jian's parents may want to press charges," the cop says. "But for now I'll drive you there."

"Please forgive me," Reba says to me as the cop leads her away. "And please keep living at my house. I'd really like you there if I have to be in care for a while."

I don't have time to process all that, because just then Lin walks in.

Chapter Fifteen

Lin stares at me lying here in a hospital bed. "Oh my god! Are you okay, Kipp?"

"Yeah, I'm fine." Our eyes meet, and we both smile. My heart races.

"Nice gown," she says. "That sick green color really suits you."

I pull the covers up over my bare legs. "Thanks! How's Jian?"

"He's out of surgery, and our parents are talking to the doctor now. It will take awhile, and he'll need a lot of physio, but he's going to be okay."

"That's great! He was in pretty bad shape when I found him."

"Yeah, we heard." She makes this face like she's both happy and sad. "Thank you so, so much for saving him."

"You're welcome. I'm glad I could help."

"That was really brave of you, going out alone with Reba."

"Yeah, well, Jian needed my help." Lin has no idea that what I was most scared of wasn't Reba, but being in her boat. And I'm not telling her. Not yet. I like that she thinks I'm brave. "Do you think Jian will come home when he gets out of the hospital? Will your parents take him back?"

"Don't know. I sure hope so, but he'll have to work something out with them."

"I hope so too." And I really hope I can see Lin again after I get out of here.

"Did that cop come?" she asks. "Did she take Reba to jail?"

"No, she took her for a psych assessment. Apparently Reba had a breakdown before, when her son went missing."

"Oh. So she won't be charged with anything?" Lin does not look impressed.

"Something like that, I guess," I say. "But I don't really know what will happen to her."

"But aren't you mad at her? Don't you want her to be punished?"

I shift my arm so the IV line is more comfortable. "Well, sure, I was mad at her. But now I'm just glad everybody is okay, and I want Reba to get the help she needs."

"Huh. I'll have to think about that." Lin looks out the window, then back at me. "What will you do now? Where will you go?"

"You can sit down if you want." I point to the chair by my bed. She does, and I tell her about Reba saying

I can still live at her place. "And I was thinking that when she's better, I might help her look for Ben."

"Wow! After how she treated you? You're way too nice!"

"Not really." I tell her about Fern and how she died. How I ran away without going to her funeral or even talking to her family. "I wasn't nice to them." Then I tell her how I promised to honor Fern's memory by making something of my life. "And I've kind of failed at that too," I say. "I don't know if I can start again."

Just then Lin's parents come into the room, smiling.

Mrs. Cheng says, "We've talked to the doctor, and everything went well. Jian had a nasty break, but they've fixed it and his leg should heal up okay. We haven't seen him yet though."

Mr. Cheng steps up beside my bed and says, "Thank you for saving Jian." He holds out his hand, but this time I'm the one who doesn't shake. Well, I can't, not with the IV in there.

I wave my left hand, and he grasps it. "My son, Jian..." he says, his voice breaking.

"Yes. Thank you for helping us find him," Mrs. Cheng says. "And we hope you're okay too." She holds out a bakery box that says, *Happy Cookies Make Happy Days*. "We brought you these."

Through the cellophane window on the front of the box I can see big, round smiley-face cookies.

"Those look great! Thanks."

Then there's an awkward silence.

Lin looks at her parents like she's waiting for them to say something more. Finally Mrs. Cheng says, "If you need a job, we have an opening at the bakery."

"Seriously? You want to hire me?"

"It's the early-morning shift." Mr. Cheng gives me a stern look. "Not when Lin works."

What have I got to lose? It's a long bus ride from Reba's, but I can manage that. "Sure. I'll give it a try." And one way or another, I'm pretty sure I'll be able to see more of Lin.

After they leave I've finally got some time to think about everything.

Could it really work out, looking after Reba's house for her and working at the Happy Cookies bakery?

Maybe.

But there's something else I need to do first.

It's six months and two weeks now since Fern died. I've got some money from the work Reba already paid me for. Not much, but enough to make the trip back to Helston Bay.

I need to go see Fern's family and tell them how sorry I am. I need to visit Fern's grave and tell her about Reba and Jian and Lin. Especially about Lin.

I need to tell Fern it's time for me to move on. But also that I'll never forget her. Or give up on my promise.

Acknowledgments

With heartfelt thanks to my readers, my family, and everyone at Orca.

Jocelyn Shipley has written several books for teens, including *Raw Talent*, *Impossible* and *Shatterproof*. Her award-winning stories have been published in newspapers and anthologies, and her work has been translated into many languages. Jocelyn lives in Toronto and on Vancouver Island.

orca soundings

For more information on all the books
in the Orca Soundings line, please visit
orcabook.com.